John Yeoman Quentin Blake's first collaboration was on the school magazine at Sidcup Grammar School. They both went on to read English at Cambridge University, after which they continued to work together in what has proved to be an enduring creative partnership in children's books.

John Yeoman spent twenty-eight years teaching, for most of that time as Head of the English Department at the Lycée Français in London. He now devotes his time to writing – stories and verse, and also song lyrics for children's radio and television – as well as indulging his passion for gardening, the theatre, classical music and opera, and reading.

Quentin Blake began his career drawing cartoons for magazines such as the *Spectator* and *Punch*, but he is now best known for his distinctive children's book illustration, and as the creator of many best-selling titles. Head of the Illustration Department at the Royal College of Art from 1978 to 1986, he is now visiting Professor. In 1987 he was awarded the O.B.E.

JOHN YEOMAN

Featherbrains

Illustrated by
QUENTIN BLAKE

PUFFIN BOOKS

PUFFIN BOOKS

Published by the Penguin Group
Penguin Books Ltd, 27 Wrights Lane, London W8 5TZ, England
Penguin Books USA Inc., 375 Hudson Street, New York, New York 10014, USA
Penguin Books Australia Ltd, Ringwood, Victoria, Australia
Penguin Books Canada Ltd, 10 Alcorn Avenue, Toronto, Ontario, Canada M4V 3B2
Penguin Books (NZ) Ltd, 182–190 Wairau Road, Auckland 10, New Zealand

Penguin Books Ltd, Registered Offices: Harmondsworth, Middlesex, England

First published by Hamish Hamilton 1993
Published in Puffin Books 1994
1 3 5 7 9 10 8 6 4 2

Filmset in Monophoto Plantin Light

Printed in England by Clays Ltd, St Ives plc

One

Flossie and Bessie lived on Fairacres Farm. At least, that was the name printed on the egg boxes. It was actually just a very long shed with a passageway running right down the middle and chicken cages piled high on either side.

Flossie and Bessie, who were sisters, shared a cage with Maggie and Aggie, two other hens. It was the one nearest the doors, on the bottom row on the right-hand side.

The shed was full of chickens; about twenty thousand of them. But they didn't talk much. When nobody's been anywhere or done anything there isn't very much to talk about.

That Thursday began like any other day.
When the lamps (there were no windows in the
shed) were turned up automatically at seven
o'clock, the hens took their heads from under
their wings and blinked a bit in the light.

"Did you sleep well?" asked Flossie.

"Yes, thank you," said Bessie. "I had a lovely
dream."

"That's nice," said Flossie. "What did you
dream?"

"I dreamt that I was in a cage in a long shed.
And then I woke up."

Flossie looked wide-eyed. She never had

dreams. Bessie was the imaginative one. "You are lucky," she said.

"Ooh, look," said Bessie. "Breakfast."

She always said that at about this time, because this was when the machinery switched itself on. First it began to hum, then it went clunk-clunk a few times, and then something even more exciting happened: the belt at the bottom of the metal channel that ran past all the cages started to move along.

After a while chicken-feed began to travel past and, by pressing themselves against the bars of the cages and standing on each others' necks in turns, the four hens were able to peck at it.

"It's the same as yesterday," said Bessie, between beakfuls.

"That's nice," said Flossie. "It was very tasty yesterday. I really enjoyed it yesterday."

They said this every day. Aggie and Maggie didn't say anything, though. They were too busy eating. They were usually too busy to talk: too busy eating, or sleeping, or staring into space.

Two

So far, then, this Thursday was just like any other day. That is, until a small, dark, glossy head poked through the gap where the doors didn't quite join, and looked around inquisitively. It was a jackdaw, and he decided to come in.

Nosiness is the jackdaw's next-to-worst fault. His worst fault is that he tends to steal things. When people take things which don't belong to them we call them light-fingered. Well, jackdaws are light-beaked. Very friendly, but very light-beaked.

He took a quick look round, hopped the whole length of the passageway, saw that there wasn't anything worth collecting, hopped all the way back again, said "Pooh!" in a choking voice, and turned to leave.

"Just look at that poor chicken," said Flossie.

"Jackdaw," said the jackdaw.

"Good morning, Jack," said Flossie. "You look terribly skinny. Doesn't he look skinny, Bessie?"

"Yes, he does," said Bessie. "You really should look after yourself, Jack. Didn't you have any breakfast? I bet he didn't have any breakfast, Flossie."

"I bet you never have any breakfast, from the look of you, Jack," said Flossie. "Come on, have a bite to eat with us. It'll do you good."

"It'll fatten you up," said Bessie.

The jackdaw was rather touched by their concern and craned his neck over the metal channel. What he saw and smelt passing by on the belt made him clap his wing over his beak.

"Thank you all the same," he gulped, "but I was just on my way to find some breakfast when I popped in. If you'll excuse me, I must be off now."

"*Find* some breakfast?" said Flossie to herself, puzzled.

8

But as he turned to go, the jackdaw noticed a
shiny metal button glinting on the side of the
cage. Now, jackdaws can't resist shiny things
and, as he couldn't believe that it was any use to
the hens, he thought he might as well have it.

With a sharp stab of his head he tried to peck
it off but – to his surprise – the button didn't
come free. He tried again, and again, and then
the metal object suddenly sprang up with a
clang, making the cage door swing open.

In panic Aggie and Maggie pressed themselves tightly against the back wall of the cage. Flossie and Bessie stood blinking in bewilderment.

Then the jackdaw had an idea. "Since I seem to have unlocked your cage, ladies, wouldn't you care to join me for breakfast outside?"

"Outside what?" asked Bessie, more bewildered than ever.

"Do you mean there's another shed behind those doors?" asked Flossie.

The jackdaw couldn't think how to explain. "Why don't you take a look for yourself?" he said. "You can always come back in if you can't find anything tasty."

Three

Once they were out in broad daylight the two sisters stood stock still, huddling against each other for reassurance.

"It's very cold out here," said Bessie. "Perhaps we ought to go back in now. We don't want to catch a chill."

"It isn't really cold," said the jackdaw, trying to encourage them. "It's just that it was so overheated in that shed. Anyway, it'll feel much warmer as the sun gets up."

This didn't make any sense to Bessie as it was always the same high temperature in the shed.

She waited until the jackdaw had started to trot away before whispering to Flossie, "I think he's a bit simple-minded, but he's trying to be helpful."

"Come on, and I'll find us some breakfast," the jackdaw called over his shoulder as he bounced this way and that.

Very gingerly, the hens picked their way between the huge lorries that were parked on the great expanse of asphalt around the shed.

"Do hurry up," the jackdaw called, "or someone will see you."

"How can we hurry up," said Flossie, "when there's no wire to hold on to?"

The two hens were so used to gripping on to the wire floor of their cage that they felt ill at ease with a solid surface under their feet.

"You don't have to grip hold of the ground," said the jackdaw patiently. "That's the good thing about the ground: you can't fall off it."

"It's all right for you," said Bessie, "but you're not thinking of Flossie's feet."

"No one knows the trouble I have with my feet," said Flossie, with a sad shake of her wattles.

"I keep telling her that she ought to have them seen to," said Bessie.

"Perhaps if you paddled them in that puddle it would cool them down," suggested the jackdaw.

"Now isn't that remarkable, Bessie," said Flossie, tiptoeing cautiously over to the puddle. "Here's a drinking trough with no upside-down bottle over it."

"I expect it's an old-fashioned sort that they have to fill by hand," said Bessie. She'd always been clever at working things out.

The sisters paddled about in the water for some time and found that it really did help to soothe their swollen feet. Perhaps the jackdaw wasn't quite so stupid after all, they thought.

Four

"Please hurry," said the jackdaw, bouncing up and down; "there are sure to be some lorry-drivers about soon. Just let me take you across the road and I'll show you a real breakfast."

"Why should a chicken cross the road?" asked Flossie.

"I give up," said the jackdaw.

"Perhaps he is a bit simple, after all," thought Bessie.

"There's quite a lot of traffic," said the jackdaw. "I really think we should fly across to that waste patch."

"Fly!" said Bessie. "You won't catch me flying. For one thing, I might bang my head on the ceiling."

"And for another thing, we wouldn't know how," said Bessie.

"Haven't you ever taken any exercise, then?" asked the jackdaw, in surprise.

"Of course," said Flossie; "every day. If you wriggle yourself into a corner position, you often get a chance to open one wing."

"Or stretch one leg," added Bessie. "Show him, Flossie."

They huddled up together again and twisted themselves around to let the jackdaw see how they did their exercises.

"But haven't you ever been able to stretch both wings at once, and flap them up and down?" asked the jackdaw. "I mean, didn't your mother ever teach you how to fly?"

Flossie and Bessie burst out laughing.

"Oh, Jack; you are ridiculous," said Bessie. "How could she? Our mother was a big electric light bulb with a great metal hat on top."

"And, anyway, she was much too busy looking after us chicks," said Flossie. "There were four hundred of us in the family, you know."

"You win. We go on foot," said the jackdaw.

18

He strode off confidently, the way jackdaws do, neatly dodging between the cars and the motorcycles.

The two hens, who were of a much more nervous disposition, anxiously tiptoed out into the road, hesitated, started to go back, turned round in circles, sat down to think, and then darted blindly across to the sound of car horns and the screeching of tyres.

They ducked under the hedge where the
jackdaw was waiting for them, with his eyes
closed.

Bessie paused to get her breath back, and then
said: "That was much easier than I'd expected."

Five

When the sisters had had a little rest, the jackdaw led them out from under the hedge and on to the plot of waste land.

"I'm sure you'll find plenty to eat here," he said.

Flossie looked around doubtfully. "I don't think so," she said.

"Oh, no, Jack," said Bessie. "There are no chicken-feed belts here. Just a lot of dirt and grass and bushes."

The jackdaw realised that he'd have to begin at the beginning.

"And that's just where you'll find something tasty to eat," he said. "You know, worms and things. Like this." And he stabbed at a little worm and held it up in his beak to show them.

"Is that what you call food?" asked Flossie.

"It's what chickens call food," said the jackdaw.

Bessie felt bold, but not too bold. "I'll eat one if you eat one first, Jack," she said.

With a flick of his beak he tossed it down his throat, closed his eyes briefly, and gave a satisfied smile. "Delicious," he said.

"There aren't any more," said Bessie, slightly disappointed and slightly relieved.

"Yes, there are," said the jackdaw. "But they're just under the surface. You have to scratch around for them. Chickens are good at that. Jackdaws aren't really built for it."

"Never mind, Jack," said Flossie; "it'll be easier for you when you're our size."

Bessie was already scratching around. Just as the jackdaw had said, she found it quite easy – and, for some reason, very exciting.

"Look at Bessie," Flossie cried; "she's dancing!"

In no time Bessie had unearthed a little tangle of worms. Summoning up their courage, the two hens each picked up one of the smallest and gulped it down.

There was a pause while they thought about it.

"You know," said Bessie finally, "they taste much nicer than food."

"You're right, Bessie," said Flossie. "But they can't be good for us, can they? I mean, they've been on the dirty ground and they don't have any special extras."

"Extras?" asked the jackdaw.

"Oh, yes," said Bessie; "our chicken-feed always has extras to make us fit and strong . . ."

". . . like bits of chopped-up beak . . ." said Flossie,

". . . and minced feathers . . ."

". . . and medicines," said Flossie.

"Why medicines?" asked the jackdaw.

"So that we don't feel unwell," Bessie explained.

"You mean, no one ever feels unwell in that shed?" asked the jackdaw.

"Oh, yes; people are ill all the time," said Flossie.

"But I'm sure they'd be much worse if they didn't have their daily medicines," said Bessie. "For all that, I'm going to try some more of these delicious worms. After all, it's only one little meal."

"That's right, Bessie," said Flossie, starting to rake around with abandon; "it won't do us any harm to have a little snack before we go back."

The jackdaw sighed and raised his eyes to the sky. They really were hopeless.

Six

After the three of them had been eating for some time they heard a rustling in the bushes. A rabbit suddenly appeared.

"Sorry," he said. "Didn't mean to startle you. Excuse me. Short of breath. Been running."

"Good morning," said Flossie.

"Good morning," said Bessie. "I must say, I like your feathers. They're very neat."

The rabbit looked at the jackdaw. The jackdaw gave a discreet wink.

"You're very kind. Sorry, can't stop. Must be off. So must you. Fox about. And he's hungry."

With that, the rabbit span round and disappeared down a hole.

"That was clever," said Flossie, starting to scratch about again.

"Come on," said the jackdaw. "Didn't you hear him say there's a fox about?"

"Oh, Jack," said Bessie, pecking at a fat beetle; "you don't want to worry about that. There's plenty of food here for everyone, no matter how hungry he is."

"He's not interested in beetles," the jackdaw yelled. "He's interested in chickens, and he's coming this way. You'd better fly!"

"I've told you before, Jack," said Flossie, through a beakful of worms, "I've never flown in my life, and I don't intend . . ."

At that moment a sharp face with pointed
ears, wiry whiskers and glistening teeth
appeared through the grass. It was the fox. At
the sight of it Flossie let out a squawk that sent
all the birds flapping from the tree-tops.

Without quite meaning to, the sisters found
themselves beating their wings frantically and
flopping around in the air.

"Back to the shed, Flossie," gasped Bessie.
"We've seen enough of the outside world for one
lifetime."

"I don't know the way, Bessie," Flossie
squeaked, swooping and mounting as she
flapped around wildly.

"Follow me ladies," called the jackdaw,
diving effortlessly in front of them, and setting
off over the traffic.

"But I'm getting giddy, Jack," Flossie panted. "The earth keeps spinning round."

"Just close your eyes and keep flapping," Bessie gasped. She always kept her head in a panic.

So, with their eyes tightly closed and their wings flapping wildly, the sisters awkwardly tumbled and turned in the general direction that the jackdaw had taken.

Seven

Too tired to flap any more, they landed in a
feathery heap on the platform of the local
railway station. They didn't hurt themselves.
Chickens never seem to hurt themselves when
they fall, because they almost always land on
their feet, or their heads.

Bessie sorted herself out and fluffed up her
feathers once or twice to calm her nerves.

"I don't believe that this is our shed, Bessie,"
said Flossie.

"Perhaps Jack hasn't got a very good sense of
direction," said Bessie. "We ought to look for
him in case he's lost."

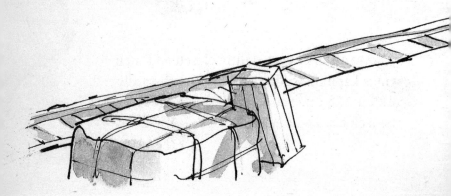

Just at that moment Flossie saw an enormous
basket on the platform, and there were bird
noises coming from it. It was a basket full of
racing pigeons, waiting to be loaded on to the
train.

Flossie jumped on to the lid and peered down
dimly through one of the air-holes.

"Now this is a lovely cage, Bessie," she said,
sadly. "All warm and cosy. And no foxes."

"I'm beginning to feel homesick," said Bessie.
"Do let's try to find Jack."

Flossie jumped down. "But I'm walking this
time," she said. "I've done quite enough flying
for one day."

34

They found the exit. Because there was no
train due for another couple of hours there was
no collector at the window, so they didn't have
any trouble over tickets.

The station forecourt was deserted, except for
a parked motorcycle with a yellow crash-helmet
hanging from one handlebar and the jackdaw
perched on the other.

"Oh, there you are, Jack," said Bessie. "You
know, we really ought to be getting back.
They'll be worrying about us."

"I wonder what the other hens are doing now,
Jack," said Flossie, wistfully.

"Not a lot," said the jackdaw. "Look; I know
that it's your home and all that, but you really
don't have to go back there. Wouldn't you
prefer . . .?"

He didn't finish because Bessie had had an
idea.

"I think I'd like to lay an egg, Flossie," she said.

"Oh, Bessie, you couldn't," said Flossie. "There's no slope for it to roll down, and no moving belt to take it away. It wouldn't be right. It wouldn't be . . . natural."

"I don't care," said Bessie, with an almost defiant tone in her voice. "You're only young once. Let's live recklessly. After all, we'll be going back home in a minute."

So they jumped up into the crash-helmet and laid their eggs.

"Do you know, Jack," said Bessie as she hopped down, "I think that was the most satisfying egg I've ever laid."

"Me too," said Flossie. "I really enjoyed that."

"And you still want to go back home?" the jackdaw asked.

"Of course," said Flossie. "We must."

"But perhaps after a little rest," said Bessie. "We've had a very tiring morning."

"You can't rest here," said the jackdaw. "Someone might see you."

"All the same, Jack; Bessie's right," said Flossie. "We need to get our strength up. It's probably a long walk back."

"That looks a nice place for forty winks," said Bessie, pointing to a little van parked further along the pavement. "It's got its back down so we can easily get in."

"It looks lovely and dark and airless," said Flossie, approvingly.

The jackdaw sighed and shrugged his shoulders, and darted up to the booking-hall roof to wait for the sisters to reappear.

He didn't have long to wait. Almost immediately there came the sound of ferocious barking, followed by the sight of Flossie and Bessie taking off at high speed to escape the snapping jaws of the guard dog.

Eight

"Follow me," the jackdaw called, launching himself into space. "I'll lead you straight back home. It won't take any time at all."

He reckoned without the hens' lack of flying experience. The fact that they kept their eyes shut and had difficulty remembering to flap both wings at once made their progress very slow.

He had to keep coming back for them.

39

Once he had to disentangle them from the
goal-net on the school playing-field.

Once he had to persuade them to get out of a
shopping trolley that was standing outside the
village stores.

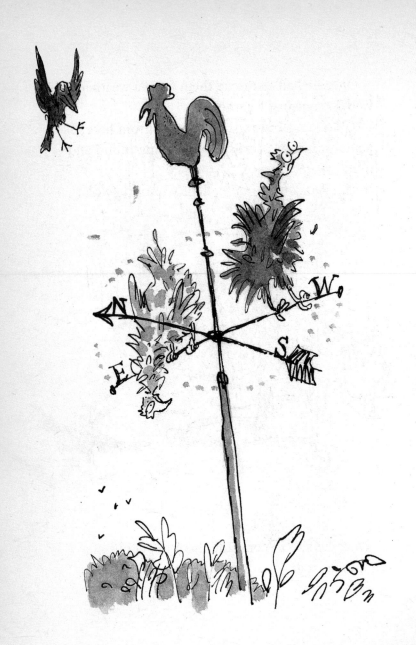

Once he had to rescue them from a weather-vane in someone's garden.

"I hope it's only a short journey from here," panted Flossie. "The ground's going round and round again."

The jackdaw waited patiently until they had sorted themselves out.

This time, by circling around them in the air and nudging them in the right direction now and then, he managed to get them to crash-land into the lorry-park of Fairacres Farm.

"There," puffed Bessie, as she tried to stick some of her loose feathers back into place, "it's not nearly as difficult as it looks."

"Just come and see us to the door, Jack," said Flossie, rather sadly, "and then we'll have to say 'thank you' and 'goodbye'."

But a great shock was in store for Flossie and Bessie. When they reached the tall double doors they saw that the gap at the bottom had been boarded up. Someone had discovered that they had gone missing and had ordered the repair.

They could never go back home.

Nine

The two sisters just couldn't believe it.

"Whatever shall we do, Bessie?" said Flossie.

"I can't think," clucked Bessie; "it's the end of the world."

"Don't be upset, ladies," said the jackdaw. "Everything may have turned out for the best, after all. There's nothing else for it now, you see: you'll have to let me show you a little place I know."

The hens looked at each other doubtfully, but they had to fall in with his plan. In less than half an hour they had completed the ten-minute flight to the spot that the jackdaw had told them about. They had to agree that it really was an attractive place: a little clearing in an oak wood.

"And with its own fresh stream, you see," said the jackdaw, bouncing over to a stone and dipping his beak in the sparkling water.

"It's got very pretty flowers in the grass," said Flossie, who didn't want to seem ungrateful.

"And there's a nice patch of dust over there for a dust-bath," said Bessie, beginning to explore.

"And there are plenty of juicy insects under all these pebbles," said Flossie, starting to scratch around.

"Do you know," said Bessie, after a pause, "I don't think it's such a bad place to stay if we can't have the real thing. Thank you, Jack."

And that night Flossie and Bessie snuggled up together at the top of a hawthorn bush and let the rooks in the tall trees send them to sleep with their cawing.

As day followed day they began to discover
new pleasures: different coloured flowers
appeared, showers of rain fell to freshen them
up, and their friend the rabbit set up home with
his family under the hawthorn bush.

The jackdaw, of course, kept an eye on them.
In fact, he went to see them every day. And he
was delighted to find that, gradually, they talked
less and less about the shed and began to take to
their new way of life.

Ten

One morning (and by coincidence it was another Thursday morning) he found the two hens taking a leisurely dust-bath when he arrived.

"Hello, Jack," said Flossie. "It's good to see you."

"Did you both sleep well?" asked the jackdaw.

"Yes, thank you," said Bessie. "I had a lovely dream."

"Ooh, tell us," said Flossie.

"Well, I dreamt I was in a clearing in a wood. And there was a cool stream trickling by. And then I woke up."

"What a coincidence," said Flossie. "I had my first dream ever last night – and it was exactly the same as yours!"

"That's nice," said the jackdaw, with a smile.

Also in Young Puffin

OLGA
Takes Charge

Michael Bond

Graham was in love. There was no doubt about it.

Olga da Polga cannot believe that her friend Graham the tortoise has fallen for someone who doesn't speak and who is so tall that he cannot even see her eyes. With her usual sense of 'sorting things out', Olga sets out to discover what's really going on in the garden.

THE Hodgeheg

Dick King-Smith

Max is a hedgehog who becomes a hodgeheg, who becomes a hero!

The hedgehog family of Number 5A are a happy bunch, but they dream of reaching the Park. Unfortunately, a very busy road lies between them and their goal and no one has found a way to cross it in safety. No one, that is, until the determined young Max decides to solve the problem once and for all...

MRS COCKLE'S CAT

Philippa Pearce

Peter Cockle longs and longs for a mouthful of fresh fish.

One of the things that Mrs Cockle's cat, Peter, loves most in the world is fresh fish for tea. One summer the weather is so bad that the fishermen can't take their boats out to sea. Peter has to do something about the lack of fresh fish...and Mrs Cockle is left all alone.